MISFIT A

When Kids Rule the School

Written by Stephanie Gee

Illustrations by Mike Motz

ISBN 978-0-9876790-0-0

Author Stephanie Gee
Illustrations by Mike Motz

Cover and Interior Design by GKS Creative

Printed in Canada

To all the kids who love to daydream...

Special Thank You
to Warren G. and Amaryah O.

Bobby Loo is in the third grade and he is always getting into trouble. Bobby Loo gets yelled at for so many things. He walks too slow, runs too fast, talks too loud, raises the wrong hand, eats too messy, and gets too dirty. He paints too sloppy, writes too neatly, reads too quickly and sings too softly.

HISTORY
School is Cool
Bobby

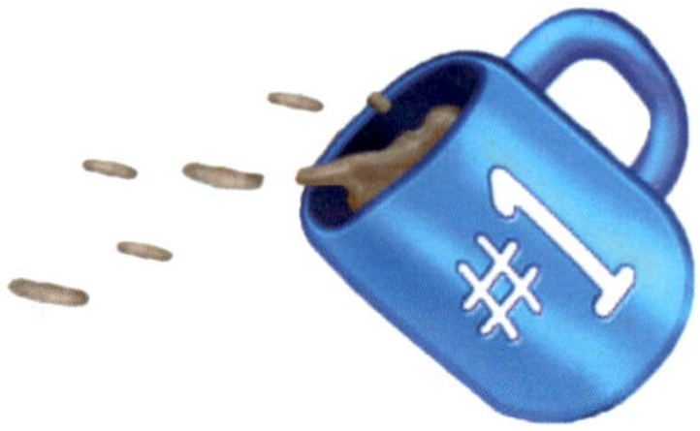

Bobby Loo is always being sent to see Principal McMeanie.
Principal McMeanie always says the same thing;
"Bobby Loo this is a school and there are rules you need to follow. Don't run, don't sing, don't talk, don't yell, don't laugh, don't cry, don't wiggle, don't giggle".

RULES
Don't RUN
Don't SING
Don't TALK
Don't YE
Don't LAU
Don't CR
Don't WIGG
Don't GIGGL
NO KID ZONE!
I ♥ DETENTION
#1
Principal McMeanie

One day Bobby Loo decides that he is feeling brave and he looks Principal McMeanie straight in the eye and says:

"Mr. McMeanie, I do NOT like your rules".

Principal McMeanie takes one long look at Bobby Loo, the hairs on his head stand straight up, his face turns bright red and it gets darker and darker until steam starts to come straight from his ears. He slams his giant fist on top of the desk, opens his mouth full of crooked yellow teeth and screams:

"Bobby Loo when kids like you run this school you can have your own rules but until then you will follow mine!"

Bobby Loo slumps back into his chair. He can't stop thinking about what school would be like if kids *could* run the school...

SCHOOL RULES
NO
RULES!
I ♥ FUN
KID ZONE!
CANDY
RACE
8
Principal Bobby Loo
8

If kids ruled the school there would be no need for principals. Kids like Bobby Loo would be in charge and the first thing he would do is tell Principal McMeanie to leave. Bobby Loo would call him into *HIS* office, point his little finger at him and say: "Mr. McMeanie, this is a school and there are rules YOU need to follow. You need to laugh and play, sing and dance, jump and run, wiggle and giggle, scream and cry. Mr. McMeanie you need to leave because you are too scary, too stinky, too loud, too old and most of all, tooooo mean!"

PRINCIPAL

With Bobby Loo in charge kids could do all the things they've dreamed about. Instead of lunchtime cleanups there would be lunchtime food fights: a meatball toss, grape squash, jello jiggle, apple juggle, pie slush, soup spit, chicken fling, fish flop, burger swap, beans in the pants and a pudding dance.

OUT
IN
MILK

Kids would be able to eat and drink whatever they wanted.
Instead of healthy snacks they could have:
marshmallow sodas, strawberry cappuccinos, cinnamon milkshakes, candy coated carrot sticks, licorice pops, chocolate pizza, ooey gooey tacos and jellybean juice.

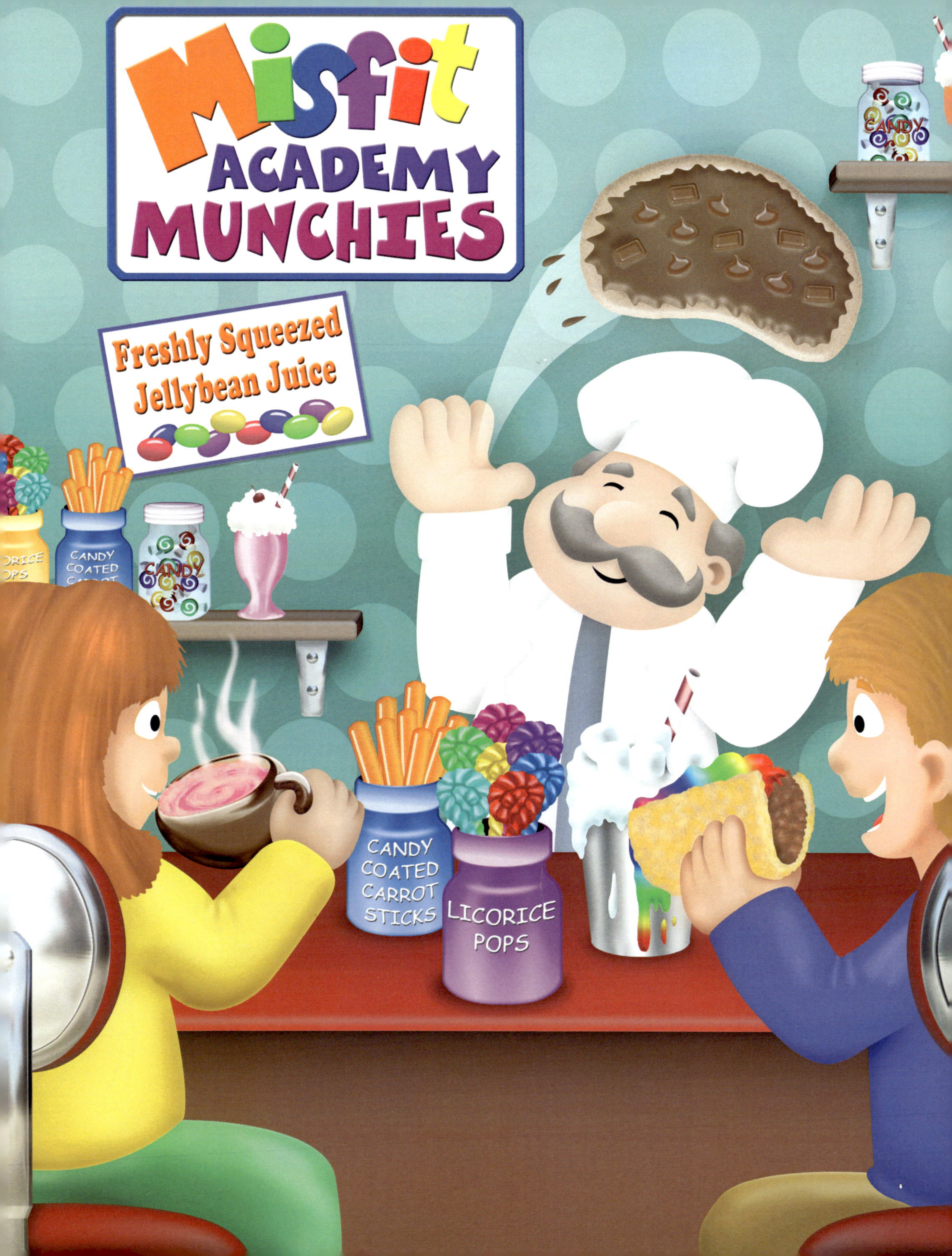
Misfit
ACADEMY
MUNCHIES
Freshly Squeezed
Jellybean Juice
CANDY
CANDY
COATED
CANDY
CANDY
COATED
CARROT
STICKS
LICORICE
POPS

If kids were in charge there would be a gigantic swimming pool right in the middle of the school. Instead of math and spelling tests, all exams would be tested in the pool: How huge we can splash, how deep we can dunk, how high we can dive, how big we can cannonball, how long we can float and how fast we can flutter. Of course, there would also be waterslides, with one super twisty slide so tall that you can choose to climb the extra large ladder or take the way-too-fast elevator.

ELEVATOR
SUPER SLIDE

Bobby Loo decided that if kids ruled the school, they'd do so in stylc. Instead of big yellow buses, kids would ride horses to school. Kids would have horses with names like Captain Cheerio, Pink Thunder, Mister Cupcake, Mighty Mini, Master Stank, Funky Fred, Silly Sally and maybe even Pretty Penny. Bobby Loo would have the biggest and brightest horse of all, called Purple Lightning, with a blue tail, yellow hairdo, shiny silver teeth and the fastest, strongest legs of all the horses in the world.

MISFIT
ACADEMY

If kids ruled the school they could decorate it however they wanted. They would paint on the walls, draw on the floors and cut and glue wherever they pleased. They would paint purple elephants, yellow alligators, fuchsia stars, violet sunshine, blue goldfish, silver bananas, gold tomatoes and pink potatoes. They would leave footprints, handprints, elbow prints, knee prints, nose prints, belly button prints and bum prints all over the school.

PRINCIPAL

In the schoolyard there would be a monster roller coaster that goes up and down and all around. On the roller coaster there would be seats for every kid in the school so nobody had to wait in line. Instead of just 15 minutes, recess would last for 3 long hours or until the kids got tired. In the park there would be swings to the sky, infinity sandboxes, mile long monkey bars, slippery slides, super size soccer balls, big bouncy basketballs, twisty skipping ropes and one extra large so-high-you-could-touch-the-sky trampoline.

8
BOBBY-LOO

If kids ruled the school field trips would be around the world.
They would take planes, trains, boats and rocket ships.
They would dig up old dinosaurs, blast off to the moon,
climb Kiliminjaro, swim with the sharks, walk through
the jungle, see the North Pole, take a trip to Timbuktu
and sail the oceans with Bobby Loo.

B U

T…

If kids ruled the school they might not have time to learn all the things they needed to know. They might never find out what 3 million 4 hundred and 63 thousand plus 5 equals. They might never learn how to spell Mississippi or how to write cursive letters. They might never dissect a frog or experiment with chemistry. They might never find out how Rome was built, or how it is that airplanes could fly. They might never learn how to play the flute or how to sing the alphabet song. But worst of all, if kids ruled the school they might never not ever learn how to read, and what a tragedy that would be!

10
5
6
13
7
Miss
DICTIONARY
8

Bobby Loo slumps back into his chair to think about all of the neat things he might miss if kids ruled the school. Just then Principal McMeanie storms back into his office. “Bobby Loo, are you *DAYDREAMING* in my office?! WAAAAAKE UP!! Bobby Loo snaps up.

PRINCIPAL
#1

"It's OK Mr. McMeanie I was thinking about strawberry cappuccinos, big shiny horses, monster roller coasters, mile long monkey bars, pink potatoes, gold tomatoes and trips to Timbuktu." Principal McMeanie takes one long look at Bobby Loo, the hairs on his head stand straight up, his face turns bright red and gets darker and darker until steam starts to come straight from his ears. But before he can say a word Bobby Loo looks at him with a smile from ear to ear, says "it could happen", and walks out whistling.

WHEN KIDS RULE THE SCHOOL: SEARCH & FIND

- Bobby Loo's 2 pet frogs
- Principal McMeanie
- Silver bananas
- The school chef
- 7 Handprints
- 4 Goldfish
- 6 Apples
- 1 Ooey Gooey Taco

Freshly Squeezed Jellybean Juice
Principal McMeanie
NO KID ZONE!
I ♥ DETENTION
isfit
ACADEMY
UNCHIES
MISFIT ACADEMY
KID ZONE!
School is Cool
#1
DICTIONARY
MILK
I ♥ FUN
Principal Bobby L
Misfit Academy RULES!
SCHOOL RULES
NO RULES!

About the Author

Stephanie Gee (Stephanie Gliksman M.Ed) was born and raised in Montreal. Stephanie is a Special Ed. Educator and has a passion for writing stories. Stephanie works in elementary schools and draws a lot of inspiration from the amazing children she encounters.

When Kids Rule the School is Stephanie's first published book. Stay tuned for more as she will be adding many more titles to the *Misfit Academy Series*.